Song of
the Giraffe

Song of the Giraffe

by Shannon K. Jacobs

Illustrated by Pamela Johnson

Little, Brown and Company

Boston　Toronto　London

First Edition

The characters and events in this book are fictitious. Any simi-
larity to real persons, living or dead, is coincidental and not
intended by the author.

Library of Congress Cataloging-in-Publication Data

Jacobs, Shannon K.
  Song of the giraffe / by Shannon K. Jacobs ; illustrated by
Pamela Johnson.
    p. cm. — (Springboard books)
  Summary: Hoping for the respect of her tribe and inspired
by a dream, Kisana braves a dangerous journey to find the
fruit of the baobab tree and a long-lost spring.
  ISBN 0-316-45555-5
  [1. Africa — Fiction. 2. Baobab — Fiction.] I. Johnson,
Pamela, ill. II. Title.
PZ7.J152537So   1991
[E] — dc20   91-438

Springboard Books and design is a registered trademark of
Little, Brown and Company (Inc.)

10 9 8 7 6 5 4 3 2 1

WOR

*Published simultaneously in Canada
by Little, Brown & Company (Canada) Limited*

PRINTED IN THE UNITED STATES OF AMERICA

For my husband, George
— S. K. J.

AUTHOR'S NOTE

Song of the Giraffe was created with great respect for all indigenous peoples. It is a work of fiction and does not depict any specific tribal traditions of Africa.

1

In Kisana's village there was no water. Every morning the women walked to a water hole an hour away to fetch water. They filled jars with muddy water, balanced the heavy jars on their heads, then walked back to the village.

Kisana, who was ten, loved to go with the women who sang and laughed, wrapped in their colorful dress cloths. She thought the women looked like beautiful water birds, with their long, bare legs and feet and their graceful, high steps. And she got lost in wishing that

she, too, were tall and graceful like her favorite animal, the giraffe.

But Kisana was very small. The rest of the people in her tribe — the Bokuru tribe — were tall. They also were dark-skinned, with chocolate brown hair, while Kisana's skin and hair were lighter. Many times she had overheard other villagers say that she was not from the Bokuru tribe.

"Of course you are Bokuru!" her mother told her angrily whenever Kisana repeated what she heard. "Your father is Bokuru. I am Bokuru. You have to be Bokuru."

"Then why am I not tall?" asked Kisana. "And why is my skin the color of ripe apricots instead of black plums?"

Her mother answered gently, "All people do not look the same, my daughter. Wataba's nose looks like the beak of a hawk. But no one accuses her of being a bird, do they?"

Kisana laughed and shook her head. Her mother laughed, too, and sent her outside to tend the garden behind the hut.

Kisana had planted the garden, and it was growing very well. Already, squash and pumpkin vines clung to the small hill, and many corn plants waved in the wind. Peas and beans grew rapidly up poles.

But there was no water. The short rains that should have come two months ago had not come. Kisana's garden, like all the others in the village, was beginning to dry up.

One night the village leader and medicine man, Suele D'Bulo, called the tribe together. "This is the worst dry spell our village has known," he told the people. "We must find water or our crops will burn up, and we will starve."

He then talked about the hidden spring that ran nearby in underground caves. They all had heard about it in stories passed down by their ancestors. But no one knew where the spring was. Somehow, over the years, the secret of the spring had been lost.

"When the new moon rises, in five days' time," said Suele D'Bulo, "we will hold a feast for the ancestors. Every person in the tribe must bring an unusual or rare gift. Then we will pray that we will learn where the spring is."

As the villagers walked back to their huts, Kisana heard them talking loudly about what gifts they would offer to the ancestors. She could not think of any special gift she could bring.

"What can I give?" she asked her mother.

"You can help me string beads. We will make a fine necklace," said her mother.

Kisana smiled at her mother's thoughtfulness, but she wished for her own special gift so the villagers would accept her with pride. If her gift was not right, though, it would bring shame upon her. As she lay down to sleep, Kisana began to dread the feast in five days.

2

The next day, as Kisana tended her garden, she noticed something struggling in the bushes a distance away. She ran to check and, with a cry, saw that it was a baby giraffe. Its leg was caught in a wire snare set for antelope. The harder the giraffe tried to kick off the snare, the tighter the trap became.

Kisana ran to her hut and grabbed a sharp knife. She hurried back to the giraffe and cut the thin wire. Just then Kisana saw Lavo, the boy who had set the trap, coming to check on

his snare. She pushed the baby giraffe away from her, and it galloped off quickly.

"You fool!" cried Lavo. "That was my gift to the ancestors — a giraffe skin."

"The ancestors would not like skins from babies," Kisana replied.

"You will pay for this, you . . . you Naba!" Lavo yelled in her face. Kisana ignored him. She was used to being called a Naba. They were a tribe of small people who lived in the bush.

She slowly walked back to her garden where the corn stalks wilted in the blistering sun. She felt happy that the baby giraffe was free, but she knew that Lavo would, indeed, pay her back.

That night Kisana dreamed about a giraffe. He said to her, "Because you saved me, I will save your people. I will show you where the hidden spring is." He led Kisana to a rocky hill, where a big baobab tree grew.

"Find the fruit of the baobab tree, and you will find your spring," he said.

In the dream, Kisana knelt down and saw a hole in the rocks. She peered in, hoping to find fresh water bubbling . . . but then she awoke.

Kisana related the dream to her mother, who was stirring porridge in a pot over the fire. "You must tell that one to Suele D'Bulo," her mother suggested.

Kisana quickly went to Suele D'Bulo's hut. He sat in the doorway, his face tight with worry. When she asked politely if she could enter, he acted as though he had not heard her. She asked again, more loudly, and he waved her inside.

After she described her dream, Kisana asked, "What does it mean, 'Find the fruit of the baobab tree and you will find your spring'?"

The old medicine man frowned and shrugged his shoulders. He could not figure it out, for he had not been listening well. "It means nothing," he said. "Go help your mother now. And do not be setting animals free when we need the food."

"But it was a baby," Kisana protested.

"Then you must harden your heart," Suele D'Bulo said impatiently. He sent her out of the hut. As she left, Kisana decided that he was right, and she forgot about her dream.

The next night, Kisana had another dream about the giraffe. This time she was tending her garden, near the squash plants, when the giraffe appeared and said two words: "Black snake." Kisana woke up but put the dream out of her mind.

Later that morning, as she watered her squash plants in the garden, Kisana saw something that made her heart stop. A black mamba — one of the most poisonous snakes in the country — was coiled underneath the plant's leaves, ready to strike. She quickly ran away.

"I must pay attention to my dreams," said

a relieved Kisana to herself.

She thought over the first dream. Now she believed its message. "I must find the baobab tree, for that is where the spring is hidden," she decided.

But the only baobab tree anyone knew about was an ancient tree that stood near the village of Ranwalo, at least a day's journey away. Kisana knew she would have to travel alone to Ranwalo. Suele D'Bulo did not believe in her dream, and he would forbid her to leave. Her mother always followed his advice when her father was gone.

Kisana quickly ran to find Paburo, to tell her friend of her plans. "Tomorrow, after I leave for Ranwalo, please tell my mother where I have gone," Kisana asked.

Paburo nodded, her eyes round with worry. "It will be a dangerous journey alone, Kisana," she said.

"Yes," Kisana agreed. "But it is the only way."

3

The next morning, Kisana awoke before dawn and dressed very quietly. She slipped a small leather pouch over her shoulder and stuffed it with her good red dress cloth, pieces of bread, and dried fruit. Then she slung a small gourd over her other shoulder. This she would fill with water when she passed a water hole.

Without making a sound, she left the hut. As she passed over a hill outside the village, Kisana heard the throaty cough of a leopard. She reminded herself to stay alert. Leopards loved the early morning for hunting, she knew, and lions who had not eaten during the night would be hungry also. Soon it became light enough to follow the dusty path leading west.

When the midday sun glared like an evil eye, Kisana stopped at a water hole to fill her gourd. She sat in the shade of an acacia tree and sipped water. It was such a hot time of day that it was hard to breathe, much less move. Kisana was beginning to think she had made a mistake.

"I should be home, stringing beads with my mother," she said to herself, "not following a dream." She decided to return home after she had rested.

The heat rose from the earth in waves, silencing the bush. She closed her eyes and leaned against the tree. She dreamed again of the giraffe.

In this dream she was trapped in a golden field, and a big lioness jumped out at her. She started to run, and the lioness chased her. Then she saw the giraffe's face rising out of the grass.

"Do not run," the giraffe said.

So she stood as still as she could. The lioness looked at her, then walked away. Kisana saw the giraffe off in the distance, watching her.

"Thank you," she called after the giraffe.

She awoke with her pulse racing. Thinking about the dream, Kisana felt a warmth inside her. This was the second time the giraffe had saved her in her dreams. It was another sign, she decided as she stood and stretched. She should continue her search for the baobab tree and the hidden spring.

Kisana had walked only a short distance when suddenly, out of the corner of her eye, she saw something running at her. Her heart leapt like a frightened gazelle.

Then she slapped her thighs and laughed loudly as she saw what it was. A baby monkey.

The monkey looked terrified. He now sat

trembling, watching her, his fingers in his mouth.

"Come here, little Wanake," she coaxed, naming him *nut* in her language since his head looked like a nut. He stared at her with big brown eyes as she offered him a dried apricot. He took the fruit, smelled it, and put it in his mouth.

"Are you all alone?" she asked, looking about for other monkeys. There were no other animals in sight. "I will take care of you, little Wanake," she said, picking up the tiny creature who clung to her as he would to his mother.

Unfolding her red dress cloth, Kisana made a sling. With Wanake centered in the sling, she tied it around her, and he rode on her back like a human baby.

For several hours she and Wanake headed west. Before Kisana knew it, the sun rested like an orange ball on the top of the mountain. She stopped, feeling quite disturbed.

"But we should be at the baobab tree by

now," she said out loud. She looked ahead but saw no signs of a village. She listened carefully but could not hear cattle lowing or goats bleating.

Kisana was very nervous. She had not planned on spending the night in the bush. And yet, here she was, alone. She knew that once the red-orange fire of the sun disappeared, it would be too dark to see her hands in front of her face. There was no darkness so deep, so black, as in the bush at night.

Noticing a small clearing nearby with three tall trees, Kisana decided to sleep there. She quickly gathered all the sticks and branches she could find and started a fire in a small circle of rocks.

As the chill of night settled over her like a cold blanket, Kisana wrapped her good red dress cloth around her and Wanake. Then, using her bag as a pillow, she lay down next to the fire. Before she knew it, she was fast asleep.

4

A *twack* sound woke Kisana. It was the edge of dawn. She sat straight up, smelling the cold ashes in the fire. She could not see Wanake.

In a moment she heard him, though. He leapt down from a tree overhead and landed, chattering with fear, near her. Kisana stood up and inspected the tree. Halfway around the large trunk she spotted what had frightened Wanake — an arrow stuck in the tree.

Of course, Kisana thought, this was the noise that woke me up. She knew the arrow meant that Naba people were hunting nearby. They were probably watching her right now.

Kisana had heard many stories about the little Naba people. They hunted with poisoned arrows, traveling in small bands. They were shy of other people and hid quickly, so few people actually saw them.

Kisana's father, Jejuba, liked the Naba people. He was the only one in the village who could speak their language. He traded food and arrowheads with them.

"The Naba are the only good people left," he had told Kisana and her brothers once. When they had asked him what he meant, Jejuba had explained, "They take only what they need from the earth. Never more. That way there is always enough."

Her father also had said the Naba were very peaceful people normally. "But," he had added, "they have learned to be fierce hunters."

"Because of the white people coming to our country?" Kisana's oldest brother had asked.

Her father shook his head. "Because of all people. Even us, even the Bokuru. We have all slaughtered the little Naba people. And sold them as slaves. Now there are few left. Maybe none. I have not seen signs of the Naba for several seasons."

That was last winter that Kisana's father had spoken about the Nabas. Now here she was, faced with hunters so skilled with bow and arrow that she stood no chance of escaping if they decided to shoot her.

But the fact that they had shot at Wanake, a baby monkey, angered Kisana. She grabbed the arrow, careful not to touch the deadly tip, and yanked it out of the tree. Holding it in front of her, she walked in the direction from which it came.

"Here is your arrow," she said. "I return it to you." She waited for what seemed like a very long time. Finally she heard a rustle, like wind stirring dry leaves on a tree. A small young man with copper-colored skin stepped

out of a shadow. Kisana never would have seen him if he had not moved.

The boy, wearing only a loincloth made of hide, carried a bow in his left hand. Arrows stuck out of a quiver on his back. His brown eyes were guarded, but he did not seem frightened as he met Kisana's angry stare. When he saw Kisana's hand tremble as she held out his arrow, though, his dark eyes warmed.

As the boy moved toward her, Kisana noticed he was exactly her height. It was a surprise to her. All the boys in her village anywhere near her age were much taller than she.

Keeping his eyes on Kisana's, the boy reached out and took the arrow with a touch so swift and light she did not feel anything. Kisana was fascinated by his face, and she felt herself staring at his high cheekbones and slanted eyes. He did not look like any other tribe she had ever seen. Yet he also seemed familiar.

The boy put the arrow in his quiver. Then he smiled slightly, his eyes crinkling at the corners in such a way that Kisana felt she could trust him. He slowly backed away from her.

"Wait!" Kisana cried. The boy stopped. She pointed to Wanake, then she pointed to herself, her heart.

"I care for him," she said. She moved her arms as if rocking a baby.

The boy's eyes lit with understanding, and he nodded. Then the boy burst out laughing.

It was the most beautiful laugh Kisana had ever heard.

The boy kept laughing until Kisana laughed, too. She imagined how funny it must look to the boy, who hunted monkeys for food, that Kisana cared for a monkey like a baby. She laughed harder. Then the boy laughed harder.

Soon they had to sit down and hold their stomachs.

Finally Kisana said, "Stop. I cannot breathe."

When they both quieted down, they stood slowly, feeling shy.

Kisana did not want the boy to leave. She wondered if they could find a way to speak to each other. She pointed to herself.

"Kisana," she said. The boy repeated her name with a smile.

Then he pointed to himself. "Xu," he said, with a slight clicking sound. Kisana repeated his name, which sounded like *zoo* to her.

Xu backed off slowly into the trees. Before Kisana had time to speak, he had disappeared without a sound.

She held Wanake tightly. "Maybe Xu was a spirit," she said softly, "a laughing spirit." She stood for a long time looking in the direction in which Xu had disappeared.

5

Still watching for Xu in the trees, Kisana gathered up her good red dress cloth and wrapped Wanake in it so he once again could ride on her back. She climbed a small hill and looked down where the Swara River cut the valley below like a giant snake. Kisana saw tall grass surrounding the dry river bed.

When she got closer to the grass, she saw it was higher than it had looked from afar. A herd of elephants could disappear easily in it. As she pushed through the tall, waving grass, it crackled and snapped under her feet.

She saw the lioness at the same time the lioness saw her. About thirty feet away, the large cat sat up, cocking her ears toward Kisana.

All the horror stories about lions flooded over Kisana in a flash, and she felt she had been drained of all her blood. As if in a nightmare, she tried to scream, but no sound came out. She tried to move, but her legs were stuck.

The lioness watched Kisana closely. She crouched low, growling, and moved closer, ready to pounce. As Kisana's legs suddenly worked, she jumped backward and turned to run.

But just then she heard a voice. "Do not move!" the voice commanded. The lioness leapt at Kisana, landing not more than ten feet away.

"Do not move," the voice repeated, and Kisana could not tell if she was asleep or

awake, for it was the voice of the giraffe from her dreams.

The lioness stood watching Kisana, swishing her tail back and forth. But Kisana pretended to be a tree. Nothing in her body moved. She prayed that Wanake would stay asleep.

Sitting, the lioness waited patiently for a twitch or sound. But Kisana was so good at pretending that the big cat became impatient. She would much rather have something lively to chase.

Standing quickly, the lioness turned and headed into the tall grass, flipping her tail back and forth. She blended completely with the golden grass and disappeared in seconds.

Kisana kept motionless as long as she could. Then she blew out a big breath and felt her legs shaking uncontrollably. She knew that if she had run, the lioness would have chased her and easily caught her for breakfast. Then she remembered the voice that had saved her.

She turned around slowly. There stood Xu,

smiling, his big brown eyes kind and warm.

"I see you," he said in greeting.

"I see you," she answered. Suddenly she recognized Xu's warm brown eyes. They were the eyes of the giraffe in her dreams.

"There are hungry animals in the grass this morning," Xu said. "Let us go carefully." And he walked past her to lead the way through the grass. She noticed that Xu did not make nearly as much noise as she did, breaking and shaking the brittle grass.

"How do you know my language?" she asked him. He smiled.

"A Bokuru man taught me," he explained. "He traded with my people."

"Is he called Jejuba?" she asked.

Xu smiled, surprised. "Yes," he said.

"He is my father," Kisana said proudly. Then she asked Xu where his people were. He nodded toward the smoke Kisana could see clearly now.

"I am traveling to the village of Ranwalo,

near the ancient baobab tree," she said. "Do you know of the tree?"

"Perhaps my grandmother can help you," he answered. "Let us ask her." And he walked quickly ahead again.

Halfway across the sandy riverbed, Xu dropped to his knees and studied the animal tracks. He pointed to a spot where it looked as though there had been a bloody struggle.

"Your hungry lion," he said, smiling. "She has hunger no more." Kisana's stomach fluttered as she thought about her narrow escape.

6

Once they reached the Naba camp, Xu led Kisana into a hut made of branches and giant leaves. Inside, an old woman sat sewing hides. Like Xu, she was small and copper colored, although very wrinkled all over. Xu spoke to her in sounds with many clicks and pops.

The toothless woman looked at Kisana. Kisana noticed her eyes were milky looking.

"This is Adu, my grandmother," Xu said to Kisana. "She is blind. But she sees."

The old woman said something in the Naba language. Xu smiled and patted the woman's arm, then translated for Kisana.

"She says the daughter of Jejuba is welcome to stay with us for as long as she wishes," he said.

"Please tell her I am very honored," Kisana answered.

Xu did so, then gestured for her to be seated near Adu. The old woman continued sewing the leather, feeling with her hands as if each finger could see.

Wanake squirmed in his sling, so Kisana untied the dress cloth and let him down. He ran to Adu and jumped on her lap. Adu laughed in surprise, then began petting him and speaking softly to him.

Kisana sat quietly on the ground next to Adu's fire, waiting for the old woman to speak again. Xu sat motionless, also waiting. The rhythm of Adu's hands as she returned to her sewing was soothing to Kisana.

Without knowing what she was doing, Kisana began humming softly, her eyes following

Adu's hands, which flew in circles like small birds. Then Kisana sang. Her voice filled the small hut as she sang her favorite song, the song of the giraffe. Her words gave thanks to the beautiful animals, free and wild, that graced the lives of people who could not fly or gallop or live in the sea.

Xu closed his eyes, his face tilted as if trying to feel every sound. His expression of joy touched Kisana's heart as nothing in her life had ever done. The feeling he inspired in her melted her fears of looking foolish. And Kisana knew there was nothing her people could do — laugh at her, tease her, torment her — that would change this memory.

When she finished her song, Xu sat quietly, smiling at her. Adu, her hands still, looked at Kisana with her unseeing eyes. The old woman laughed as tears spilled down her face, and she wiped them with the back of her hands. She spoke to Xu, and he translated for Kisana.

"You have given her a beautiful gift," Xu said. "She says she was able to walk through the bush again and see the lovely animals, thanks to you. And, for a very special moment, she saw her totem animal, that which she loves above all. The giraffe."

"I, too, love the giraffe," said Kisana. "And I am happy my song pleases Adu." She paused, not wanting to be rude, but needing to find the baobab tree — and the spring — soon.

"Please, Xu," Kisana asked. "Can Adu tell me where the ancient baobab tree is?"

Xu spoke to his grandmother, who shook her head. She talked to Xu rapidly.

Xu turned to Kisana. "There is no more baobab tree," he said. "It died the winter past." He saw the disappointment on Kisana's face and said gently, "I am very sorry, Kisana."

7

Xu's gentleness broke the dam. Kisana found herself weeping in front of strangers when she would not allow herself to weep in front of her own family. Without speaking, she uncovered all her wounds — the names she had been called, her tiny size and light skin that would never attract a Bokuru husband — and her need to find the hidden spring. All of it came out in waves of weeping until she felt very tired.

Adu touched her arm. Looking at her two

kind friends through tear-filled eyes, Kisana felt gratitude. Xu translated for Adu as Kisana told them how the giraffe in her dream had directed her to find the fruit of the baobab tree.

She stood up, ready to leave. But Adu reached for her hand. She spoke to Xu, whose face broke into a radiant smile.

"She will give you the 'fruit of the baobab tree,'" Xu said.

"But the tree is dead," protested Kisana.

Adu patted Kisana's hand, then led her to a bag hanging from the back of the hut. She reached inside it and brought out a large, fuzzy pod, about the size of a foot. While Xu translated, Adu spoke.

"This is the last fruit from the baobab tree. I saved it to plant another. You can now plant the seed of the ancient tree," Adu said.

"The last one? I am not worthy of this!" exclaimed Kisana, holding the pod as if it were sacred. When Xu expressed this to his grand-

mother, she gave a little shriek and spoke loudly.

"She who is visited by giraffes in the world of dreams is more than worthy of this small gift," Xu said quickly, trying to keep up with his grandmother.

He continued, "You are honored by your dreams, Kisana. And you have earned them."

After Kisana had thanked Adu, she prepared to leave. But suddenly Wanake clung to the old woman as if she were his mother. Kisana asked Adu if she would like to keep the little monkey. Adu nodded her head and petted him.

Then she thanked Kisana with a hug. She said something to Xu in Naba, and he laughed.

"What did she say?" asked Kisana, always concerned about people laughing at her.

"She said you seem very tall," Xu explained, his eyes crinkling. Kisana laughed, too. No one had ever thought she was tall before.

Then Xu added, "And I told her you were

also very beautiful." Pleased but embarrassed, Kisana lowered her eyes and smiled.

Xu walked with her for awhile. When they reached the Swara River, he stopped.

"Go well," he said.

"Stay well," she answered.

Kisana turned quickly and walked toward the rising sun, in the direction of her village. A moment later she turned back, but there was no sign of Xu. A feeling of dizziness passed over her, as she wondered if he had ever existed. But when she felt the weight of the baobab fruit in her pouch, she knew he was real.

8

All day Kisana walked home, singing aloud. She had not found the hidden spring, but at least she now had a special gift for the ancestors. And she had made friends she would never forget.

As she neared her village at dusk, she saw many men and boys arriving also. Her heart quickened, for that meant her father and brothers were home. Usually they worked far away, in town, to earn money for the family.

Running as fast as she could, Kisana reached

her hut in no time. She leapt through the door, startling her family members, who were seated on the floor, eating. In one bounce Kisana landed in her father's arms. He hugged her hard, very happy to see his only daughter.

"Look at you, a grown woman," said her father. She laughed and told him how much she had missed him. Then she remembered that she had not been home for two days. She glanced fearfully at her mother, expecting harsh words and punishment.

"I went to find my gift for the ancestors, Mother," explained Kisana. "I could not tell you yesterday. I was afraid you would forbid me."

"It was your good fortune that your brothers arrived home early. They helped me with chores today," her mother said, hands on her hips. She tried to look stern, but Kisana could tell she was relieved.

"I am grateful to you," Kisana said, turning to her brothers. Just then she saw her youngest brother grab her leather bag.

"Do not touch that!" she cried. "It is my gift to the ancestors."

But her brother ran out of the hut and crashed right into Lavo, the boy who had vowed to pay Kisana back for setting the baby giraffe free. Lavo grabbed Kisana's bag and laughed.

"Perhaps I should guard this for you," he said to Kisana, walking off with her bag.

"Come, children, bring your gifts," said Kisana's mother as loud drums announced the beginning of the feast. Kisana stood still, too surprised to speak, while her family hurried to get ready.

The drums beat louder, and Kisana's family carried their gifts to the center of the village, where a huge fire blazed.

All the villagers gathered, the women in their brightest dress cloths and beads, the men painted in beautiful designs. Around and around the fire they danced. Suele D'Bulo,

with his spectacular hyena mask, led the dancers.

After the dance, Suele D'Bulo called to the villagers. "Bring your gifts to the ancestors," he said.

Each family laid their offerings at Suele D'Bulo's feet. Many women had done bead-work with colorful designs. Many men had brought animal skins and lions' teeth.

Kisana almost cried out when she saw Lavo lay down his gift. Then she saw it was a beautifully carved antelope horn.

"Where is my bag?" she whispered as he passed by her. But he only smiled.

Kisana's family was last. Her father laid down the finest arrowheads he had ever made, a true treasure for the ancestors. One by one her brothers added rich works of leather, and her mother set down a beautiful necklace of beads strung with ostrich eggshell pieces.

Then it was Kisana's turn. She didn't know

what to do. She looked for Lavo in the crowd but could not see him.

"Kisana!" a voice called.

She turned around. Lavo dropped her bag and lifted his foot.

"No!" she cried, just as his foot pounded the leather bag, crushing the ancient baobab fruit.

9

"What gift have you brought, Kisana?" Suele D'Bulo asked kindly. Kisana turned back to him. Something in his voice reminded her of Xu's grandmother, Adu.

She lifted herself as tall as she could, for, after all, had Adu not said she was tall? And she smiled with a new confidence, for had Xu not said she was beautiful?

The crowd had become quiet. The people were curious about Kisana's gift, since it was

taking her so long. Everyone peered at her hands, expecting to see a gift.

But she surprised them all, just as she surprised herself. Her gift was not in her hands. It rose from her lips.

As if it had golden wings, her voice soared above the crowd. She sang her song of the giraffe, the most beautiful gift she could give.

Kisana heard only quiet as the crowd listened closely, enchanted with her song. Then she heard singing. The entire village was caught up in her song, sending it skyward on millions of wings to the ancestors.

On and on the song traveled through the night. The people danced, ate, and slept to Kisana's song of the giraffe.

Suele D'Bulo went into a trance and sat down by the pile of beautiful gifts, trying to learn what to do. Then, toward morning, he cried, "Follow me!"

With his eyes fixed straight ahead, Suele D'Bulo quickly led the people to a hill nearby. It was the same hill that the women crossed over every day as they walked to the water holes.

"Kisana," he called. "Is this the hill of your dream?"

She ran to catch up with him, to the very top of the hill where poison bushes grew around a cluster of large rocks. Remembering her dream, she pointed to the rocks.

"There," she said. "That leads to the spring."

"The ancestors have spoken!" cried Suele D'Bulo.

The men used their spears to dig through the poison bushes no one would touch before. Then the villagers entered the cave. It was very cool inside and smelled wet. Soon, shouts of joy could be heard echoing from the mouth of the cave, for they had found a very large underground spring of sweet, fresh water. It bubbled from the heart of the earth and pooled into a small pond.

"The spring will flow forever!" announced Suele D'Bulo. And the people jumped into the pool of cool water and washed off dust that had been on them for months. They splashed and laughed and cried to think that the spring had been there, all the time, beneath their feet.

10

From that day on, Kisana felt that she was an important part of the village. The people treated her with the respect due someone who had saved them. They never teased her again about her size and light skin color.

Kisana did not grow taller or darker. She simply grew older. But after her experience with the Naba people, she felt tall and beautiful. And that was how she acted.

Years later, after Kisana had left the village to marry Xu, from the Naba tribe, the people

told many stories about her song of the giraffe and how it had saved the village. Once, Mataday, a young girl who had never seen Kisana, asked Suele D'Bulo what Kisana looked like.

Suele D'Bulo, the village leader and medicine man, sat back on his heels and stuck out his bottom lip, closing his eyes.

Then he said, "Ah, yes. What did Kisana look like?" He paused, as if seeing a vision.

"She was a woman of great beauty," he answered a few moments later. "I remember, especially, that she had the grace and elegance of a giraffe.

"Yes," he said with a smile, "that is the Kisana I remember."

Other Springboard Books® You Will Enjoy, Now Available in Paperback:

Angel and Me and the Bayside Bombers
  by Mary Jane Auch
The Hit-Away Kid by Matt Christopher
The Spy on Third Base by Matt Christopher
A Case for Jenny Archer by Ellen Conford
Jenny Archer, Author by Ellen Conford
A Job for Jenny Archer by Ellen Conford
What's Cooking, Jenny Archer? by Ellen Conford
Wonder Kid Meets the Evil Lunch Snatcher
  by Lois Duncan
The Monsters of Marble Avenue
  by Linda Gondosch
Impy for Always by Jackie French Koller